Published by Hachette Partworks Ltd
ISBN: 978-1-906965-52-5
Date of Printing: March 2011
Printed in Singapore by Tien Wah Press

Disney

ATLANTIS

THE LOST EMPIRE

Disney

Hachette

Milo Thatch knew Atlantis was real. His grandfather Thaddeus had spent his life looking for the lost city. Now Milo was doing the same.

An expert in languages and maps, Milo was giving a speech about Atlantis. He held up an ancient Viking shield that had led him to an important discovery.

"*The Shepherd's Journal*, the key to finding Atlantis, lies not in Ireland, gentlemen, but in Iceland." Milo paused. "Gentlemen, I'll take your questions now." He waited.

But his pretend audience of masks remained silent. Instead, the phone rang. Someone who worked upstairs at the museum barked that the boiler needed fixing. Milo sighed and whacked the boiler with a wrench.

He hoped his *real* speech would convince the museum board to fund a trip to Iceland. If he had *The Shepherd's Journal*, it would lead him to Atlantis.

Then Milo got a message. His meeting with the museum board members had been moved – and he'd just missed it! Milo grabbed his maps. He chased after the board members, who were leaving the museum.

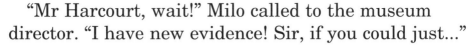

"Mr Harcourt, wait!" Milo called to the museum director. "I have new evidence! Sir, if you could just..."

But the director jumped into his waiting car. "This museum funds expeditions based on facts, not folklore," Mr Harcourt snapped. "Besides, we need you here. With winter coming, that boiler is going to need a lot of attention."

Then the car sped away, leaving Milo alone with his maps and theories.

Discouraged, Milo expected to go home to his cat, Fluffy. Instead, a mysterious woman named Helga was waiting in his apartment. She was there on behalf of her employer, who had an offer for Milo.

"Are you interested?" Helga asked.

Milo was soon in the mansion of Preston
Whitmore. He was surprised to see the old
millionaire doing yoga stretches. But Milo was
shocked when Whitmore gave him *The Shepherd's
Journal*!

"Your grandad bent my ear with stories
about that old book," the millionaire said. Milo's
grandfather and Whitmore had been good friends.
They had even made a bet – if Thaddeus ever found
the journal, Whitmore would pay for his expedition
to Atlantis. Thaddeus had finally found the book,
but he had died soon after.

But Whitmore was determined to keep his promise. Now, the expedition was ready to go. Whitmore had a submarine ready. He had even selected the crew.

"Got the best of the best," Whitmore told Milo. "The same crew that brought the book back from Iceland. All we need now is an expert in gibberish. What do you say?"

Milo could hardly believe it. He was finally going to find Atlantis!

A few days later, Milo
was aboard a ship meeting
Commander Rourke, leader of
the Atlantis expedition. Helga
was his second-in-command.
They were getting ready to
board a sleek submarine that
was loaded with machinery
and supplies.

"Boy, when you settle
a bet, you settle a bet!"
Milo told Whitmore as he
waved goodbye.

Once the sub had been launched, Milo showed slides of a giant monster to the crew. "This is an illustration of the Leviathan, the creature guarding the entrance to Atlantis," he explained. "It's a mythical sea serpent."

Soon after... CRASH! Something huge smashed into the submarine!

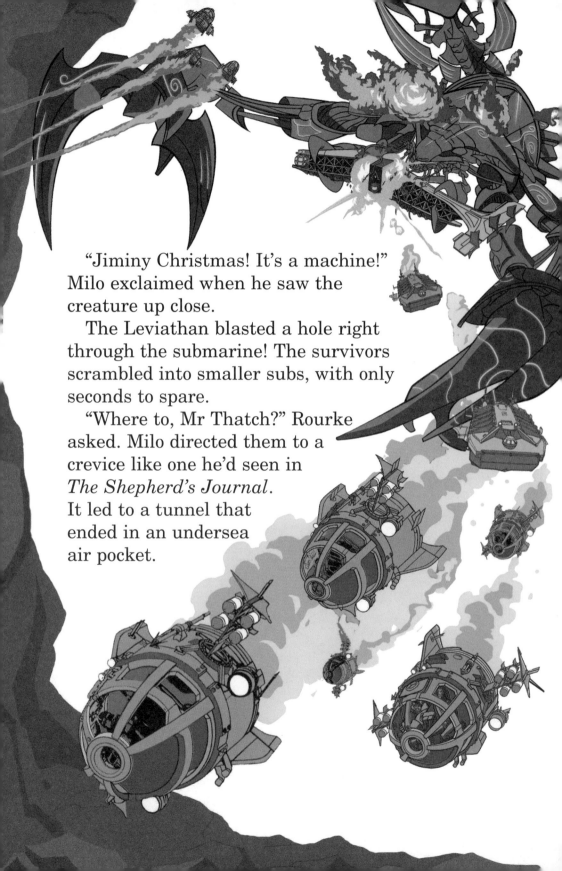

"Jiminy Christmas! It's a machine!" Milo exclaimed when he saw the creature up close.

The Leviathan blasted a hole right through the submarine! The survivors scrambled into smaller subs, with only seconds to spare.

"Where to, Mr Thatch?" Rourke asked. Milo directed them to a crevice like one he'd seen in *The Shepherd's Journal*. It led to a tunnel that ended in an undersea air pocket.

The crew unloaded
trucks and other
machines onto the dry
land. They seemed to be in a cave at
the edge of Atlantis. But they still had
a long way to go.

Rourke said, "From here on in, everyone
pulls double duty. Everyone works.
Everyone drives."

Milo wasn't much of a driver. So his truck
ended up being towed by the powerful digger
driven by Mole, the dirt-loving geologist.

But Milo proved his worth when the digger broke down.

"I don't understand. I just tuned this thing up this morning," said Audrey, the crew's teenage mechanic.

When Audrey went to get more tools, Milo whacked the engine with a wrench. It sprang back to life, just like the boiler back at the museum.

Audrey was so impressed she punched Milo – twice. As Milo rubbed his arm, he missed seeing the strange masked figures who were watching them.

That night as they camped, Milo studied *The Shepherd's Journal* alone. Some of the crew invited Milo to join them.

"Don't you ever close that book?" Audrey asked.

"You must have read it a dozen times by now," added Sweet, the medical officer.

"I know," said Milo, "but this part doesn't make sense." Milo explained that the book spoke about the Heart of Atlantis. It could be the power source that gave the Atlanteans energy, advanced medicine, and even flight. "But the book just cuts off, as if a page is missing..."

"Relax, kid. We don't get paid overtime," interrupted Vinny, the explosives expert.

Soon the crew went to sleep. But when Milo woke up in the middle of the night, his light also woke up some fireflies. These were no ordinary fireflies. In seconds, they had set the entire camp ablaze!

The crew members jumped into their trucks to escape. But the fireflies continued to attack.

KA-BOOM! A fuel truck exploded! The trucks tumbled off a bridge into a deep hole. They landed in the soft ash at the base of a sleeping volcano.

Milo was separated from the others. When he
opened his eyes, he saw the masked warriors
staring at him. He tried to sit up, but winced
and clutched his shoulder. One of the warriors
lifted her mask, revealing a woman's face. She took
a crystal from around her neck and put it on his
wound. Instantly, Milo was healed!

Suddenly, trucks rumbled towards them. The
warriors fled.

The other crew members had decided they couldn't go back the way they came. So Mole used the digger to plow through the wall of the cave. Milo was waiting on the other side, staring at the lost city of Atlantis!

Soon the masked warriors jumped out and surrounded them.

"Holy cats! Who are these guys?" Rourke gasped.

"They've gotta be Atlanteans," Milo said.

"That's impossible!" cried Helga.

But the Atlanteans *were* real. The warrior who had healed Milo took off her mask. Milo tried to speak to her in Atlantean. But amazingly, the Atlanteans spoke English and many other languages, too.

The woman, Princess Kida, gestured to the magnificent city behind her. "Welcome to the city of Atlantis. Come. You must speak with my father."

The crew climbed into their trucks and followed the warriors. Milo babbled excitedly as they crossed the bridge leading to the city. He and his grandfather weren't crazy. Atlantis *was* real, and Milo was on his way there!

Helga turned to Rourke and quietly said, "Commander, there weren't supposed to be any people down here. This changes everything."

Rourke's already stern face hardened. "This changes nothing."

Princess Kida took Milo, Rourke and Helga to her father. In the throne room, Kida argued with the king. Milo struggled to translate their rapid speech.

"You know the law. No outsiders may see the city and live!" the old king declared.

"Father, these people may be able to help us," Kida said. The proud king stiffened. "We do not need their help."

Eventually, the king agreed to let them spend one night.

After the crew members had left, Kida helped her tired father into bed. "Your heart has softened, Kida. A thousand years ago, you would have slain them on sight."

"A thousand years ago, the streets were lit, and our people did not have to scavenge for food at the edge of a crumbling city." Kida sighed. "If these outsiders can unlock the secrets of our past, perhaps we can save our future."

The king shook his head. "You will understand when you take the throne."

All Kida knew was that something had to change or Atlantis would die!

Later, Milo, Rourke and Helga spoke to the rest of the crew.

"Kida seems to like us, but the king... I think he's hiding something," Milo said.

"Someone needs to talk to that girl," Helga added.

Rourke agreed. "Thanks for volunteering, Thatch!"

Milo went to meet with the princess again. The two were full of questions for each other. Kida brought Milo to a quiet spot where they could talk.

"How did Atlantis get down here?" Milo asked.

Kida remembered the fall of Atlantis. The sky had gone dark, and a bright star had called her mother to it. "I never saw her again," Kida finished.

If Kida remembered that, Milo realized, then she was thousands of years old! But even more shocking was the fact that none of the Atlanteans could read. That's why Kida needed Milo's help.

She showed Milo a giant stone fish. It was a vehicle, but Kida couldn't read the instructions to make it work. Together, they were able to make it fly... until it crashed.

So Kida showed Milo the rest of the city on foot. Milo was amazed. "You know, Kida, the most we ever hoped to find was some crumbled buildings, maybe some broken pottery. Instead, we find a thriving, living city."

Kida shook her head sadly. "Our culture is dying." To explain, she led Milo to a deep pool.

They dived in and swam to underwater ruins painted with scenes of ancient Atlantean history. Using the light from Kida's small crystal, they saw a picture of a giant Crystal.

When they reached the surface, Milo gasped. "The Heart of Atlantis!" The giant Crystal was the Heart of Atlantis and the power source that the journal had referred to. Kida and all the Atlanteans wore a piece of the original Crystal. It was keeping Atlantis and the people alive.

"Then where is it now?" Kida wondered.

Someone else wanted to know the same thing.
When Milo and Kida emerged from the pool, Rourke
and the crew met them. Rourke pulled the missing
journal page from his boot. The crew quickly
captured Kida.

Milo suddenly knew the truth. "This is just another
treasure hunt for you. And you're after the Crystal!"

Milo felt sick. If Rourke took the Crystal, Atlantis
would die!

But the crew didn't care. They had come a very long and dangerous way, and they wanted their treasure! With Kida held hostage, Milo was forced to translate the page. But it made no sense. "'The Heart of Atlantis lies in the eyes of her king,'" he read.

Rourke's troopers blasted into the king's chamber. They grabbed the king. Rourke shook his fist at the old man. "How about it, chief? Where's the Crystal chamber?"

"You will destroy yourselves," the king warned.

Rourke sat down on the throne. Then he smiled. He could see a light shining in a pool. In it was a group of rocks forming a symbol, just like the one in *The Shepherd's Journal*.

Rourke waded into the pool and stood on the rocks, which formed a platform. He forced Milo, Helga and Kida to join him. The water trembled and the platform lowered them into another chamber below.

In the chamber, the group saw a huge, blue Crystal floating in the air above a peaceful pool. Large carved stones encircled the Crystal.

Kida recognised the faces on the carved stones and dropped to her knees. "The kings of our past!" she cried.

Rourke restlessly kicked a stone into the pool. The Crystal's light suddenly changed from blue to bright red! Search beams blazed throughout the chamber, as if the Crystal had awakened.

One of the beams of light enveloped Kida! In a trance, she walked into the pool.

"What's happening?" Rourke demanded.

Milo shrugged. "All the journal says is that the Crystal is... alive somehow. It's their power source. They're part of it, and it's part of them."

Kida spoke in Atlantean. "All will be well, Milo Thatch. Be not afraid."

Just then the great Crystal opened. A bright light lifted Kida and she was absorbed into the Crystal. Soon she returned, glowing with the light. Somehow Kida had joined with the Crystal.

Before long, Rourke had Kida locked in a transport pod and loaded onto his truck.

"So I guess this is how it ends, huh?" said Milo. "You're wiping out an entire civilization, but, hey, you'll be rich," Milo angrily shouted to Rourke.

Hearing Milo's words, some of the crew decided not to go along with Rourke's evil plan.

Rourke climbed onto his truck. "Fine. More for me!"

As Rourke, Helga and Rourke's troopers left with Kida, the Atlanteans' crystals started to dim. To make sure no one could follow, Rourke blew up the bridge behind him.

Just then Sweet called to Milo. The doctor had
been tending to the dying king. "There's nothing
more I can do for him," Sweet reported sadly.

"What a nightmare," Milo moaned. "And I
brought it here." The king handed Milo his crystal.
Then he said, "Kida has been chosen, like her
mother before her. In times of danger, the Crystal
will choose a host, one of royal blood, to protect
itself and its people."

The king continued. "The Crystal thrives on the collective emotions of all who came before us. In return, it provides power, longevity and protection." The king explained that he had used the Crystal as a weapon, which had led to Atlantis' downfall. With his last breath, the king gasped, "Return the Crystal. Save the city. Save my daughter."

Milo took the king's crystal and ran out of the palace. Now it was up to him to save Atlantis.

Milo showed the crew and Atlanteans how to make the stone fish fly using their crystals.

"Hey, Milo," Vinny called. "You got something sporty... ya know, like a tuna?"

The stone fish fleet lifted into the sky. Milo shouted, "Now let's do it!"

They caught up with
Rourke at the volcano. He
and Helga were escaping
up through the volcano's
shaft in a hot air balloon.
Kida was in her transport
pod, which was attached to the
balloon with chains.

A fierce battle broke out
between Rourke's troopers and
the stone fish fleet.

Milo suddenly knew what to
do. "Vinny, new plan: you and
me, we're gonna be decoys. Sweet,
Audrey..."

"We're on it!" Sweet cried. He
and the young mechanic tried to
cut Kida's pod loose.

As Milo jumped aboard the balloon, his stone fish ripped a hole in the balloon's side. It began to sink. Rourke tossed Helga overboard to lighten the load!

From the ground, Helga fired at the balloon, which burst into flames! Meanwhile, Milo and Rourke fought furiously. Milo managed to scratch Rourke with a piece of energised glass from Kida's pod. Rourke was turned to crystal! At the same time, Kida's pod broke free! Milo jumped to the ground and pushed the pod to safety.

The balloon exploded, causing the volcano to erupt. Cracks began to form, and hot molten lava began to flow.

"The volcano... she wakes!" Mole screamed.

Milo grabbed one of the chains on the pod. He hooked it to the tail of Sweet and Audrey's stone fish.

"We gotta get Kida back, or the whole city will die!" he shouted.

At last they reached Atlantis, and Milo prised
open the pod. Kida floated out. Protective stones
rose up and began to spin all around her. Beams of
energy burst from Kida, waking the giant statues
that surrounded Atlantis. The statues clapped their
huge hands, creating an energy dome over the city.
When the massive wave of lava arrived,
it rolled harmlessly over the dome!
Atlantis was saved!

Kida was restored to her former self.
"Atlantis will honour your names forever," she
later told the departing crew as they posed for
one last picture.

The other crew members felt sad about
saying goodbye to Milo.

"Are you sure you want to stay?" Sweet
asked him.

Milo grinned. "I hear there's an opening
down here for an expert in gibberish!"

Back at Whitmore's mansion, the millionaire spoke with the crew. He wanted to be sure Atlantis' secret would never be revealed. "Now let's go over it again," he said. "You didn't find anything?"

"Nope. Just a lot of rocks... and fish... little fish. Sponges," Vinny fibbed.

"What about Milo?" Whitmore asked.

"Went down with the sub," Audrey offered.

Whitmore sighed. He held a note and an Atlantean crystal from Milo. "At least he's in a better place now," the millionaire said.

And indeed Milo was! Way down below the ocean, Milo watched as a carving of Kida's father rose to join the other kings of the past that were protecting the amazing city.

Finding Atlantis had taken every ounce of Milo's strength, courage and cleverness. And as he held the princess's hand, Milo knew the adventure had been worth all that – and more!